W9-AMT-250

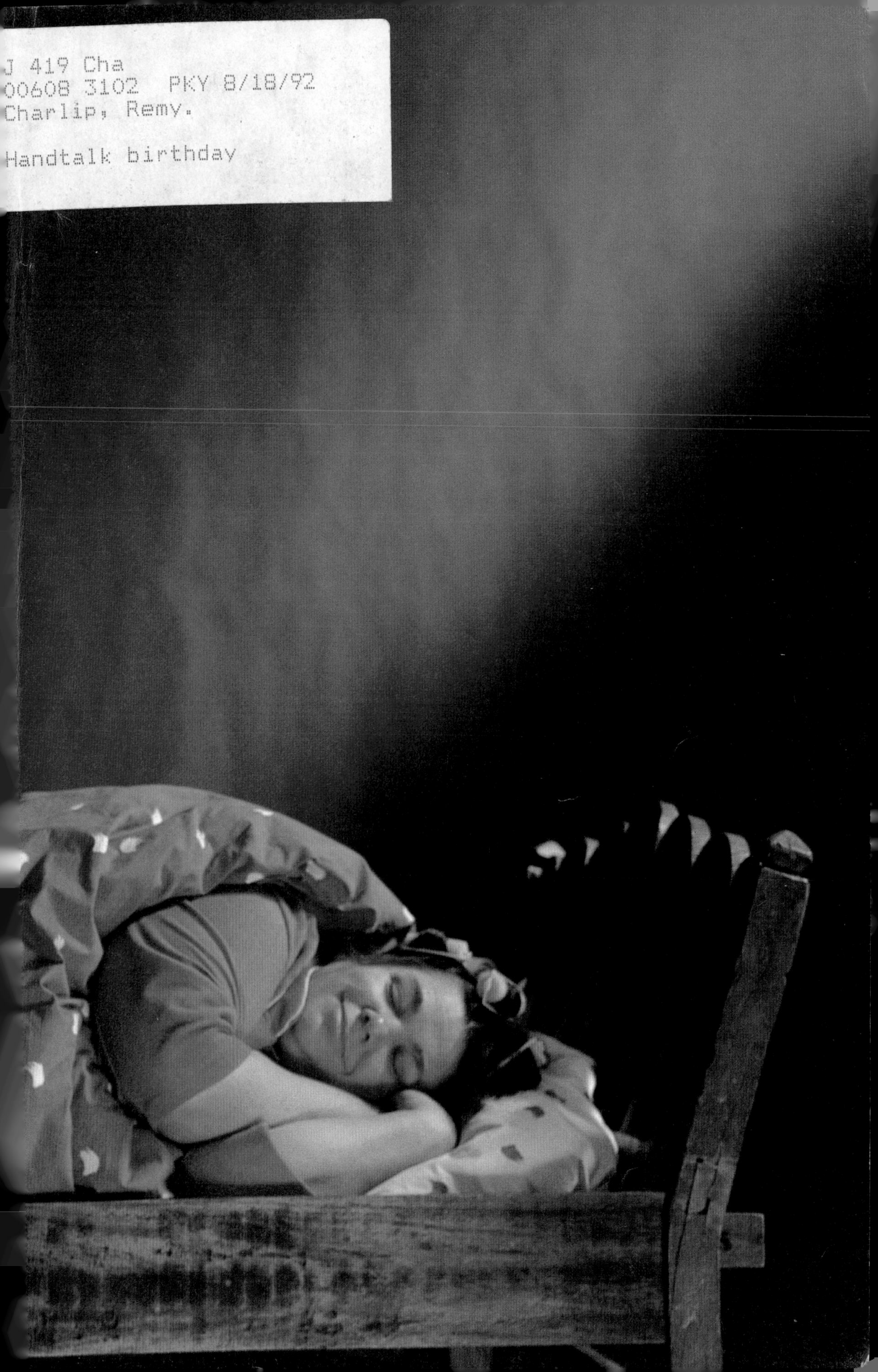

IN A DEAF PERSON'S HOME, LIGHTS FLASH AS A DOORBELL.

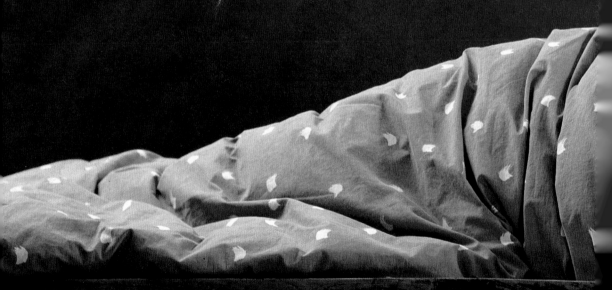

THIS BOOK IS DEDICATED TO ALL THE DEAF CHILDREN OF THE WORLD.

THANKS TO THOSE WHO APPEAR IN THIS BOOK: SETH BRAVIN, STACY NOWAK, MARTIN STERNBERG, LYNNETTE TAYLOR, JONATHAN TURNER AND FANNY YEH; AND TO THOSE WHO HELPED: PAULA BENTON, PHIL BRAVIN, MARY ANN KLEIN, DEBORAH MATTHEWS, BOB MATTHEWS, CATHY MARKLAND, MARCIA NOWAK, JANICE RIMLER, JAMES K. ROSS, VALERIE ROSS, AND DAVID AND JO ANN WEINRIB.

HANDTALK BIRTHDAY

A NUMBER & STORY BOOK IN SIGN LANGUAGE

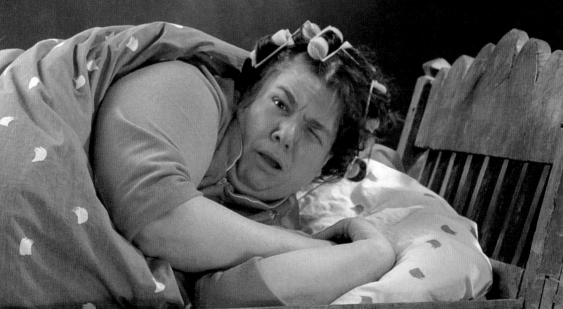

REMY CHARLIP   MARY BETH   GEORGE ANCONA

Aladdin Books   Macmillan Publishing Company   New York
Collier Macmillan Canada   Toronto
Maxwell Macmillan International Publishing Group
New York   Oxford   Singapore   Sydney

Library of Congress Cataloging-in-Publication Data

Charlip, Remy. Handtalk birthday: a number & story book in sign language / Remy Charlip, Mary Beth, George Ancona.—1st Aladdin Books ed. p.   cm. Summary: Words and sign language depict friends helping a deaf woman celebrate her birthday. ISBN 0-689-71531-5 [1. Deaf—Fiction. 2. Physically handicapped—Fiction. 3. Birthdays—Fiction. 4. Sign language.] I. Mary Beth. II. Ancona, George. III. Title. [PZ7.C3812Han   1991] [E]—dc20   91-1967   CIP   AC

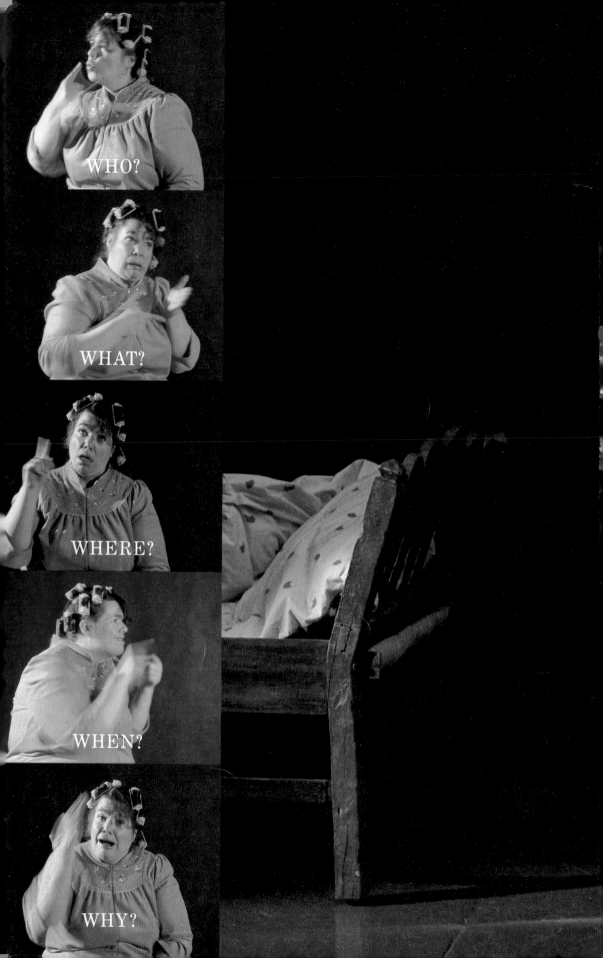

WHAT'S INSIDE?

A BALL?

NO.

FIVE

PIZZAS?

CAN

OF

T

U

I

GIVE UP.

DRUM?

NO.

NO.

A BIG

N

A

FISH?

NO!

TELL

ME.

OPEN IT!

A HAT!

THANK YOU.

A BASEBALL BAT?

A HOT DOG?

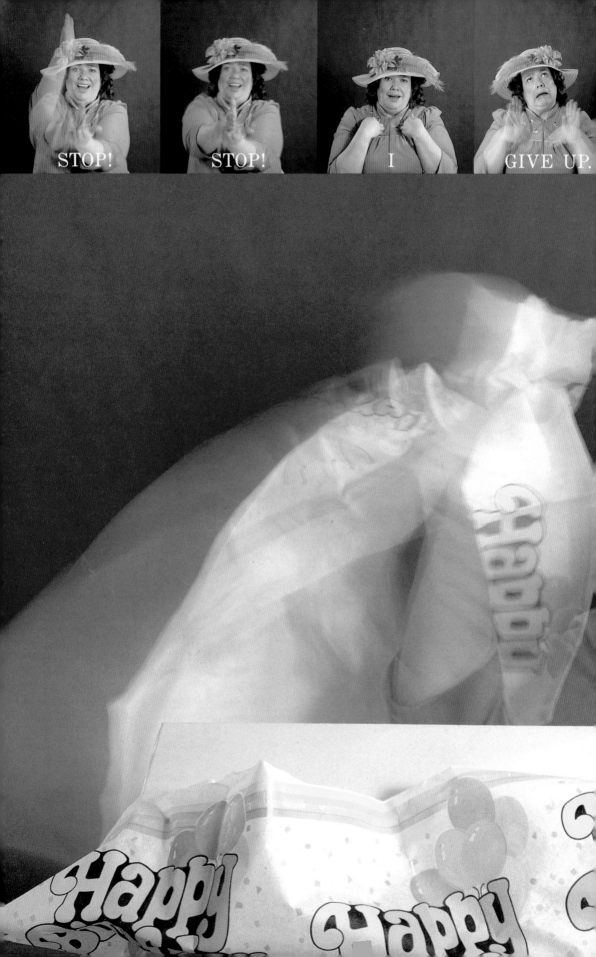

STOP! STOP! I GIVE UP.

YOU'RE   DRIVING   ME   CRAZY.

A FEATHER

BOA,

AND

IT   MATCHES   MY   HAT!

MORE?

HAPPY BIRTHDAY

HAPPY BIRTHDAY · HAPPY

GREAT! HAPPY BIRTHDAY!
ALL TIME BEST! TOP 10! WOW!

A RING?

A BOOK?

A CAT?

A T-SHIRT?

ROLLER SKATES?

GLOVES?

A WATCH?

A RADIO?

A ROBOT?

TV?

NO!

A PARTY!

PUNCH

CAKE

COOKIES

Happy Birthday

HAPPY   BIRTH   DAY

HAPPY   BIRTH   DAY

HAPPY   BIRTH   DAY

HAPPY   BIRTH   DAY

TO

YOU

TO

YOU

M A R Y

DEAR B E T H

TO

YOU.

MAKE

A

WISH

I   WISH   I   COULD

CAREFUL.

COME DOWN.

FOR

THAT!

DO YOU

HOW OLD

THINK

I AM?

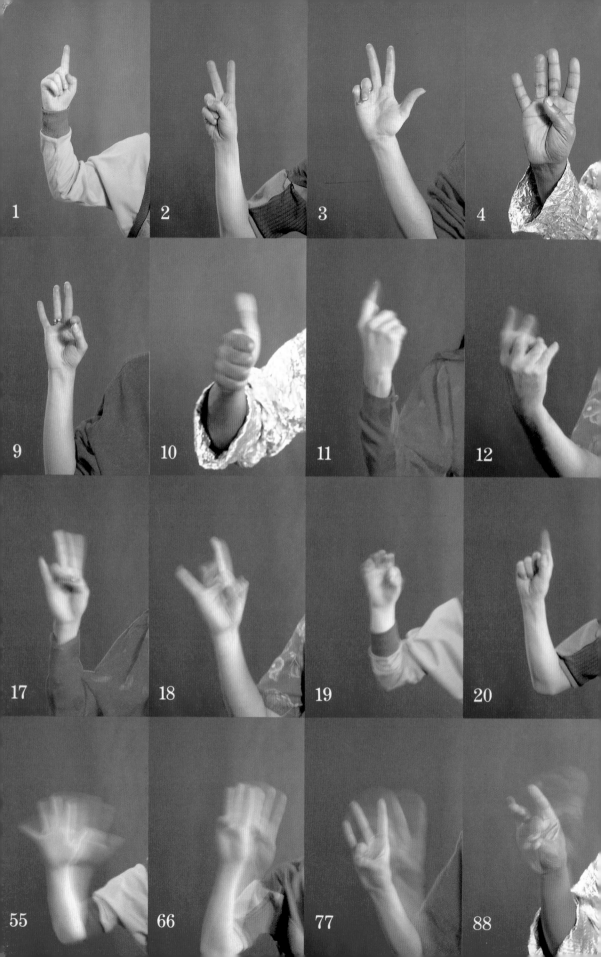

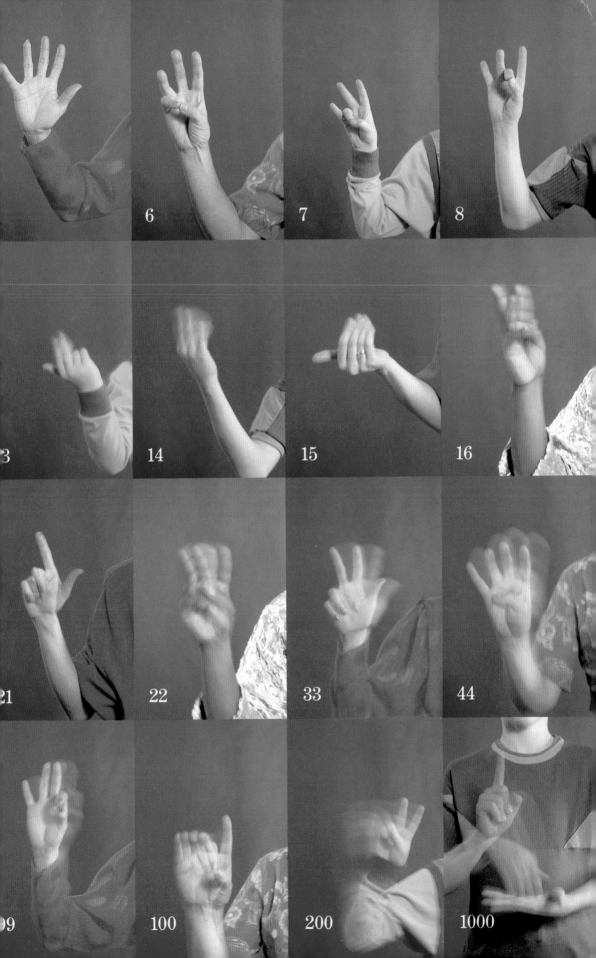

6

7

8

3

14

15

16

21

22

33

44

09

100

200

1000

MY SECRET!

43

3

40

3

BYE!

13

33